For Susanne, with love – R.E.
For Natasha Fenton, with love – S.W.

First published in Great Britain in 2003 by
Frances Lincoln Limited, 4 Torriano Mews,
Torriano Avenue, London NW5 2RZ

www.franceslincoln.com

British Library Cataloguing in Publication Data
available on request

ISBN 0-7112-2096-4

Printed in Singapore

1 3 5 7 9 8 6 4 2

Good Night, Copycub

Richard Edwards
Illustrated by Susan Winter

FRANCES LINCOLN

It was a busy summer day. Copycub and his mother spent hours in the woods, playing and nosing about for food. Copycub chased his mother. His mother chased Copycub. They tickled each other. They dug in the ground for roots to eat. His mother found a root and crunched it up. Copycub found one too.

That night Copycub felt tired out
when he lay down on his bed
of leaves in the bear cave.
But when he closed his eyes,
he couldn't get to sleep.
    He turned over one way,
but the bear cave floor felt lumpy.
    He turned over the other way,
but the bear cave floor felt bumpy.

He curled up to his mother's side, and got too hot.

He rolled away from his mother's side, and got too cold.

He lay on his back. Then he lay on his front.

Then he lay on his back again.

And at last, with all his wriggling, he woke his mother.

She yawned. "What's the matter, Copycub?"

"I can't sleep," Copycub said.

"Do you want a story?" his mother asked.

"Yes please," Copycub said. He loved stories.

His mother began.

"Once upon a time there was a small bear called…"

"Copycub!" the small bear said happily.

"That's right. And do you know why he was called Copycub? Because he was always copying, that's why."

"Who did he copy?"

"Well, listen and I'll tell you," said his mother.

So Copycub snuggled up and listened.

"One night," his mother said quietly, "Copycub couldn't get to sleep. He tried everything. He turned over one way, then he turned over the other way, and with all his wriggling, he woke up his mother. So what do you think they did?"

"What?" the small bear asked.

"They went for a walk in the moonlight."

"Copycub and his mother walked
slowly down the hillside in the warm
summer night. Everything was quiet.
Millions of stars sparkled in the sky
and a full moon was shining,
making the night as bright as day.
The bears came to a stream
and followed it through the woods
until they reached a lake.
And there, a little way from the shore,
they saw something white floating
on the water."

"What was it?" Copycub asked.

"A goose," his mother said. "A white goose
sleeping with its head tucked under its wing."
"Fast asleep?" Copycub asked.
"Safe and sound," his mother whispered.
"What happened then?" said Copycub.

"Then the two bears turned from the lake, and padded softly over the grass to the edge of the forest, where they saw a big dark shape in a clearing."

"What was it?" Copycub asked.

"A moose," his mother replied, "sleeping in the shadows."

"Fast asleep?" Copycub asked.

"Safe and sound," his mother whispered.

Copycub yawned. "And what did the bears do then?"

"They started to walk back up the hill towards their cave
when they saw something curled up in the grass."

"What was it?" Copycub asked.

"A hare," his mother replied, "a brown hare sleeping in the moonlight."

"Fast asleep?" Copycub asked.

"Safe and sound," his mother whispered.

"And when they got back to their cave, Copycub's mother asked him a question."

"What question?" said Copycub.

"Who's good at copying?" his mother replied, coming to the end of her story.

"I am!" Copycub answered.

"Yes, you are," his mother said.
"So if you ever can't get to sleep,
just think of the white goose sleeping
on the lake, and the moose sleeping
under the trees, and the hare fast
asleep in the grass…"

"And copy them?"

"That's right, Copycub."

The small bear closed his eyes.
He thought of the animals
in the story, all sleeping
safe and sound.

"I'll copy them," he murmured.

"Good night, goose.

Good night, moose.   Good night, hare."

And soon, Copycub was fast asleep too,
floating in his dreams like a goose
on a starry lake. Safe and sound.
  "Sleep well," whispered his mother,
kissing the top of his head.
"Good night, Copycub."